D0229624

CNM Duplicate

Also by G X Todd

Defender

HUNTED

GX TODD

HEADLINE

First published in Great Britain in 2018 by
HEADLINE PUBLISHING GROUP

1

Cataloguing in Publication Data is available from the British Library

ISBN 978 1 4722 3312 7 (Hardback)
ISBN 978 1 4722 3313 4 (Trade paperback)

Typeset in Bembo by Avon DataSet Ltd, Bidford-on-Avon, Warwickshire

Printed and bound in Great Britain by Clays Ltd, St Ives plc

Headline's policy is to use papers that are natural, renewable and recyclable
products and made from wood grown in well-managed forests and other
controlled sources. The logging and manufacturing processes are expected to
conform to the environmental regulations of the country of origin.

HEADLINE PUBLISHING GROUP
An Hachette UK Company
Carmelite House
50 Victoria Embankment
London EC4Y 0DZ

www.headline.co.uk
www.hachette.co.uk

For my brother, Andrew, and his wonderful family
– Sonya, Isabelle, Scarlett, and Nancy.

You make me proud to be a sister and an aunt.